This book belongs to

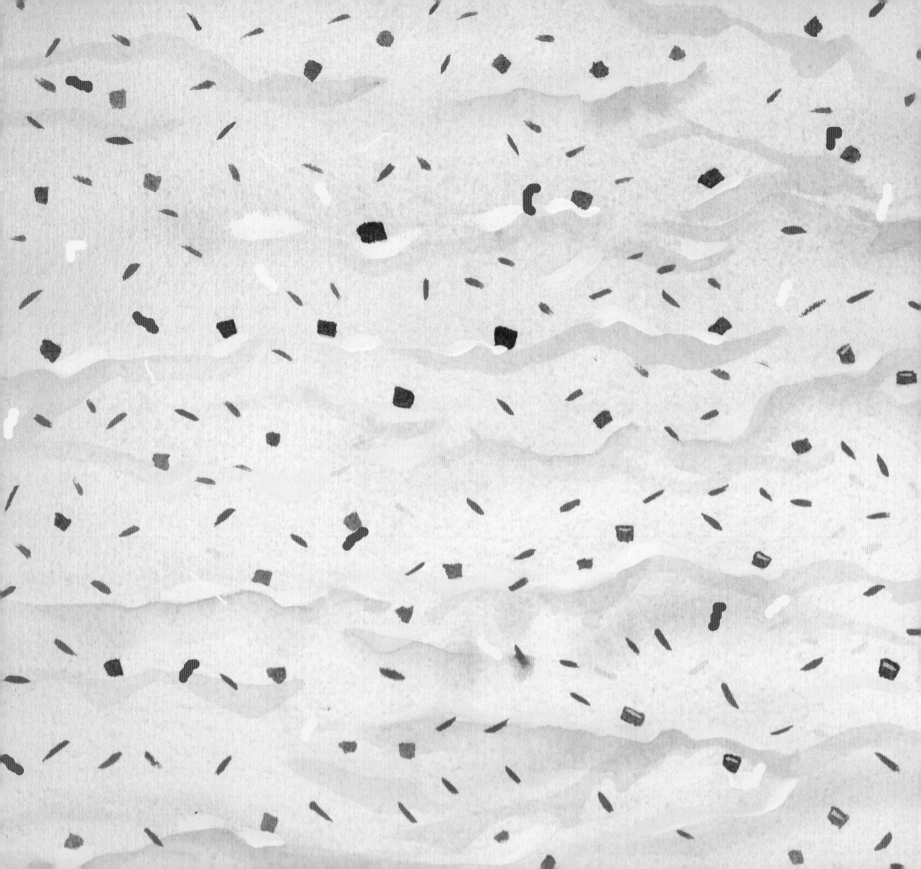

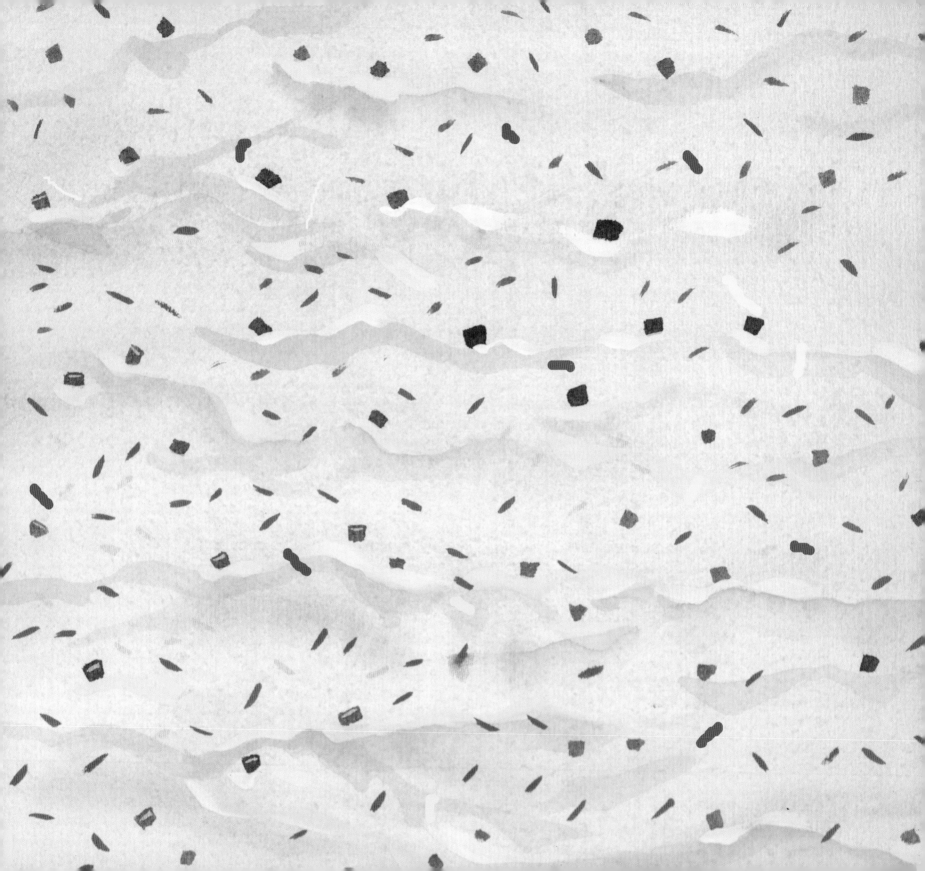

To the memory of Mutti, my beloved grandmother –*S.M.*

To Anna, the ice cream queen –*J.D.*

tiger tales

an imprint of ME Media, LLC

202 Old Ridgefield Road, Wilton, CT 06897

Published in the United States 2011

Text copyright © 2011 Steve Metzger

Illustrations copyright © 2011 Julie Downing

CIP data is available

Hardcover ISBN-13: 978-1-58925-096-3

Hardcover ISBN-10: 1-58925-096-6

Paperback ISBN-13: 978-1-58925-427-5

Paperback ISBN-10: 1-58925-427-9

Printed in China

LPP 0610

1 3 5 7 9 10 8 6 4 2

For more insight and activities, visit us at www.tigertalesbooks.com

THE ICE CREAM KING

by Steve Metzger

Illustrated by Julie Downing

tiger tales

On a hot day in July, Teddy Jones saw something that stopped him in his tracks.

"Look, Mom!" he exclaimed. "It's a **brand-new ice cream shop!** Can we go in? Can we, *please*?"

"Sure," said Teddy's mom.

Inside, Teddy looked at all the flavors on the big board. "Can I have anything I want?" he asked. "Just for me?"
"Yes," said Teddy's mom. "Anything you want— just for you."

FLAVORS
Moon Crater Crunch
Peanut Butter Party
Double Double Fudge Fudge
Raspberry Rocket
Cookie Dough Castle
Marshmallow Mountain

As Teddy tried to decide,
the server put a paper crown
on his head, and . . .

WOW! That's awesome, Teddy thought.
My mom said, "ANYTHING!"
Upon my throne of ice cream cones...
I am the Ice Cream King!

Ice cream treats are all I see—
and they're all for me!

Inside my ice cream castle,
I slide down chocolate halls.
I pick out rainbow sprinkles
from mint-chip ice cream walls.

I slip and slide down Whipped Cream Lane,
then climb up Ice Cream Mountain.

I splash and dance and spin around
beneath my ice cream fountain.

Aboard my silver sailboat,
I sail an ice cream sea.
I fish for nuts and cherries—
they're all for me, me, ME!

My very own volcano
shoots out vanilla fudge.
Today's the Ice Cream Festival,
and I'm the only judge.

I think there's something missing,
as I look around my throne,
and suddenly I notice that...

I am all

alone!

I dance and slide on ice cream.
I can even wear it.
But it would be much better
with somebody to share it.

Teddy took off his crown. . . .

"So, have you decided?" asked Teddy's mom.

"Yes," he said. "Please give me a banana split with strawberry and chocolate ice cream and lots and lots of hot fudge and whipped cream and sprinkles and . . . and . . ."

"And?" asked Teddy's mom.

"And?" asked the server.

"And . . ." Teddy said.

"Two spoons!"

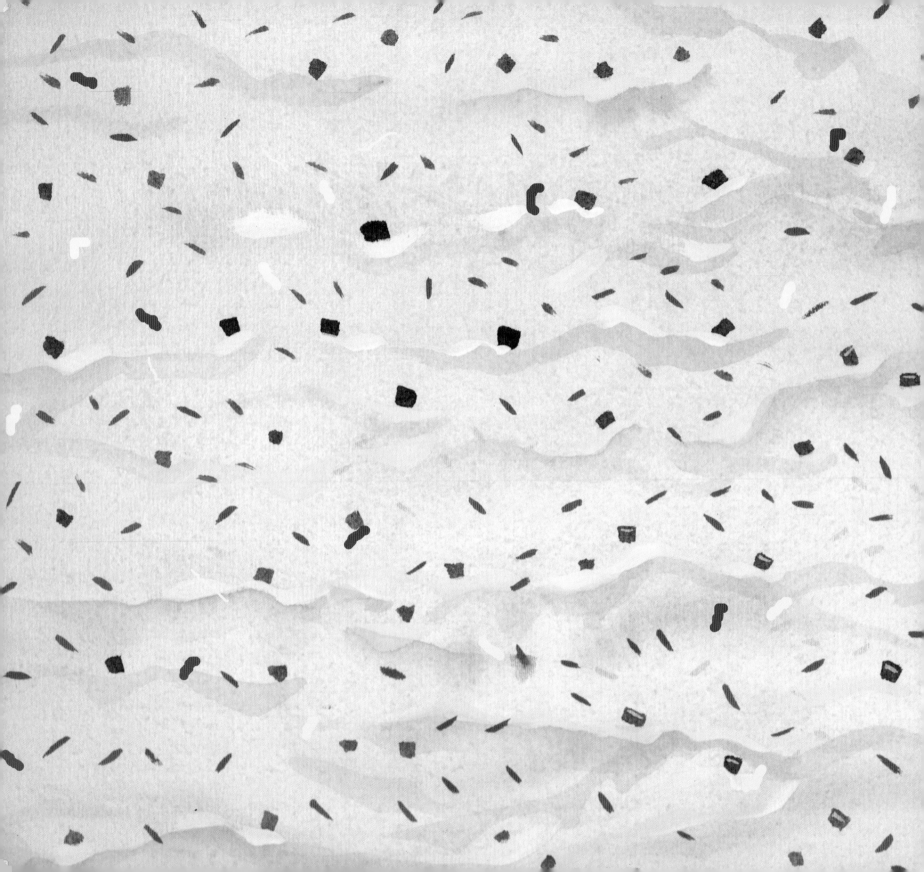

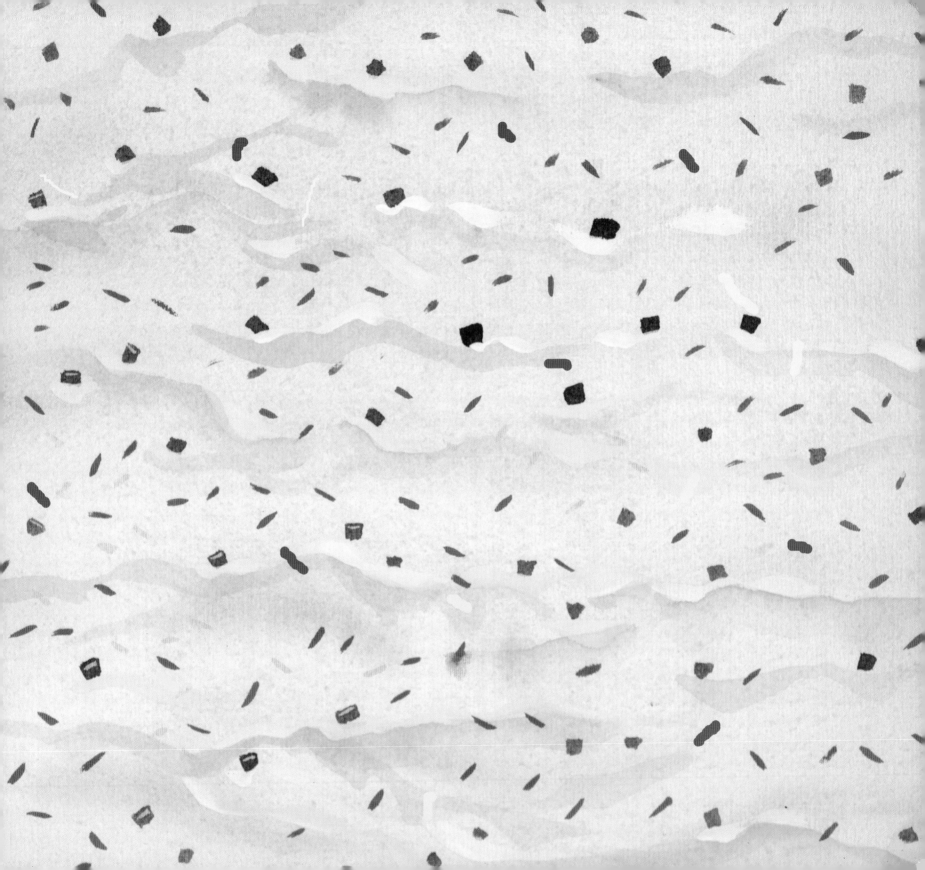

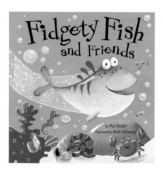

Fidgety Fish and Friends
by Paul Bright
Illustrated by Ruth Galloway
ISBN-13: 978-1-58925-409-1
ISBN-10: 1-58925-409-0

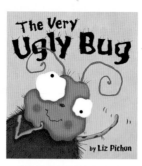

The Very Ugly Bug
by Liz Pichon
ISBN-13: 978-1-58925-404-6
ISBN-10: 1-58925-404-X

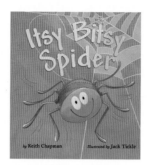

Itsy Bitsy Spider
by Keith Chapman
Illustrated by Jack Tickle
ISBN-13: 978-1-58925-407-7
ISBN-10: 1-58925-407-4

The 108th Sheep
by Ayano Imai
ISBN-13: 978-1-58925-420-6
ISBN-10: 1-58925-420-1

Explore the world of tiger tales!

More fun-filled and exciting stories await you!
Look for these titles and more at your local library or bookstore.
And have fun reading!

tiger tales

202 Old Ridgefield Road, Wilton, CT 06897

Good Night, Sleep Tight!
by Claire Freedman
Illustrated by Rory Tyger
ISBN-13: 978-1-58925-405-3
ISBN-10: 1-58925-405-8

Boris and the Snoozebox
by Leigh Hodgkinson
ISBN-13: 978-1-58925-421-3
ISBN-10: 1-58925-421-X

A Very Special Hug
by Steve Smallman
Illustrated by Tim Warnes
ISBN-13: 978-1-58925-410-7
ISBN-10: 1-58925-410-4

Just for You!
by Christine Leeson
Illustrated by Andy Ellis
ISBN-13: 978-1-58925-408-4
ISBN-10: 1-58925-408-2